THE GREAT HAMSTER HUNT

The
Great Hamster Hunt

by Lenore and Erik Blegvad

HARCOURT, BRACE & WORLD, INC., NEW YORK

also by Lenore and Erik Blegvad

MR. JENSEN AND CAT
ONE IS FOR THE SUN

To the young on the hill

Nicholas wanted a hamster.

Mother said no to that.

"But Tony has a hamster," Nicholas said.

"Oh?" said Mother. "Then go next door and look at his."

"I don't think your mother likes little furry creatures," Father remarked.

"Well, Tony's mother doesn't either," Nicholas told him. "And *they* have one."

7

Mother sighed. "Then Tony's mother is just nicer than I am," she added. "Right?"

"I guess so," said Nicholas sadly.

One day Tony came to the door.

"We're going away for a week," he said to Nicholas's mother. "Do you think Nicholas would take care of my hamster for me if I asked him nicely?"

Nicholas jumped up from his chair.

"You don't have to ask me nicely," he shouted. "The answer is *yes*!"

So Tony's hamster came to stay with Nicholas for a week. Its name was Harvey. It lived in a shiny cage with wire on top and a front sliding wall of glass. There was also a wheel that went around and around when Harvey ran inside it. On the side of the cage was a water bottle with a tube for Harvey to drink from.

Before Tony left, he told Nicholas how to take care of Harvey.

"You have to change the cedar shavings in the cage every few days," he said. He had brought a bag of them with him. He had also brought a bag of special hamster food, which was made up of fourteen different kinds of seeds and nuts. "You can give him lettuce or carrot tops, too," Tony said. "But never, never give him any meat."

"Why not?" Nicholas asked.

Tony explained that, if hamsters were fed meat, they would get to like the taste of it so much they would try to eat each other when there was more than one hamster in a cage.

"That's called being 'carnivorous' or 'flesh eating,' " Tony said. "A hamster should stay 'herbivorous,' which is 'plant eating.' "

"Oh," said Nicholas. "Wow!" He would be very careful not to give Harvey any meat. "Can I take him out of his cage?" he asked as Tony was leaving.

"Sure," Tony said. "But watch out he doesn't disappear. So long." Then, halfway across the garden, he called, "Hey, I forgot to tell you. Hamsters are nocturnal, in case you didn't know. So long."

"What's that mean?" Nicholas called back. But Tony had already gone.

All that week Nicholas took good care of Harvey. He fed him and played with him and cleaned his cage carefully. But he always remembered that Harvey was Tony's hamster. He would hold it in his hand, feeling its little cold feet on his palm and its warm, quivering fur, and he would whisper, "Oh, I wish I had a hamster just like you!"

Harvey seemed to sleep most of the day, but at night he loved to run around and around inside his exercise wheel.

Nicholas loved the squeaky noise of Harvey's wheel. It put him to sleep at night just like a lullaby.

"Yes, I wish I had a hamster just like Harvey," Nicholas said sadly to himself.

All too soon the week was up. Tony would be coming home the next evening. After supper Nicholas decided to clean Harvey's cage for the last time. He took it down to the kitchen. First he put Harvey in a large carton, where he could watch him. Then, very carefully, he slid out the glass panel from the cage, and very carefully he started to put the glass on the kitchen table, but all of a sudden…

CRASH!

The glass slipped from his hands and broke into a million pieces all over the kitchen floor!

Nicholas's father helped to sweep them up.

"We'll have to find some way of keeping Harvey in his cage until we can buy another piece of glass tomorrow morning," he said.

He found a piece of heavy cardboard, cut it to the right size, and slid it into the place where the glass had been. It worked very well.

When they had finished, it was time for Nicholas to go to bed. He was very sad because it was Harvey's last night in his house. He let Harvey play outside the cage for a longer time than usual. At last he put him in the cage and looked at him through the wires on top.

"Good night, Harvey," he whispered. "We sure had a good time, didn't we?" Then he turned out his light and soon fell asleep to the sound of the squeaking exercise wheel.

When morning came, Nicholas woke up early to have as much time as possible with Harvey before Tony came back. He looked in through the top of the cage to say, "Good morning," but...would you believe it? *The cage was empty!*

"Oh, no!" Mother said when she heard.

"Ho ho," Father said when he went to see. "He's chewed a hole right through the cardboard. And I guess we are going to have a grand time finding him!"

So they began to look—right then, before breakfast. They looked under Nicholas's bed. They looked in his dresser drawers. They looked in his closet and in all the boxes in the closet and in all the pockets of all the clothes in the closet. They looked in the toy soldier box and behind the curtains and under Nicholas's pillow and in between his blankets and inside his phonograph and even in his slippers.

When they had not found a trace of Harvey, Father sat down on Nicholas's bed.

"He could be anywhere, you know," he said gloomily. "Not just here in your room."

"And we'll never find him before Tony comes back," Nicholas said, and looked as though he might cry.

"What *are* we going to do?" Mother asked.

All at once, Father seemed to have the answer.

"We must go on a hunt for him," he said firmly. "As if he were a lion. Or an elephant. We must bring him back alive! And to do that, we must trap him." He jumped up. "First," he continued, "I'll need lots of plastic wastebaskets," and he looked at Mother.

"There's that little one in the bathroom," Mother said helpfully.

"No, no," Father said. "We must have lots more." And he dressed very quickly and rushed out of the house.

While he was gone, Nicholas and his mother continued to look for Harvey. They were still looking when Father came back with eight plastic wastebaskets. He also brought a new piece of glass for Harvey's cage.

"I borrowed the wastebaskets from the owner of the hardware store," he explained. "He was very interested in my plan."

"I can imagine," Mother said. "So am I. What is it?"

But Father was too busy to answer. He put a small pile of books in the middle of each room in the house and leaned a wastebasket against each pile so that the baskets were half lying, half standing.

"Now," he said, "I need blocks, long wooden blocks, Nicholas. And towels," he said to Mother. "Plenty of towels. And don't forget the lettuce."

"No," said Mother. "How could I forget the lettuce?"

So Father took the blocks and the towels and the lettuce and he made...

Hamster traps!

This is a hamster trap.

"Now, all we have to do is to wait for Harvey to eat his way up the ramp and fall into one of the wastebaskets," Father explained. "The plastic is too slippery for him to climb out." And he started to read his morning paper.

Mother looked at Nicholas.

"Do you think...?" Nicholas began.

"Not really," Mother said, and picked up her purse. "We'd better take a little shopping trip, just in case."

Mother took Nicholas to the pet store.

"We need a hamster, please," she said. "White, with pink eyes and a pink nose. About four inches long."

"I'm sorry," the pet store owner said. "We have only brown hamsters at the moment. Will they do?"

"No, no," Mother said. "They won't do at all.

Thank you. We'll have to try somewhere else."

And they did. They tried many other places until quite late in the afternoon.

Mother telephoned Father from the next town where she and Nicholas had finally gone on their search.

"Father hasn't caught anything," she reported to Nicholas.

"And we haven't found another white hamster for Tony," Nicholas said, again feeling as if he might cry. "Now we'll have to buy him a brown one that won't even look like Harvey."

But when they got to the last pet shop, they were delighted to see a hamster that looked very much like Harvey. It was white with pink eyes and a pink nose, and it was just about four inches long, if you did not count its extra-long whiskers.

"That's the one," Mother said, and took out her purse. The shopkeeper put the hamster in a little cardboard box with air holes punched in top. Nicholas held it carefully on his lap on the way home. He felt much better now. At least Tony would have a hamster that could remind him of Harvey.

When they got home, Nicholas put the new hamster in Harvey's cage, which they'd taken to the kitchen. It ran around in Harvey's treadmill a few times. Then it curled up in a corner of the cage and went to sleep.

"I hope Tony will get to like you as much as he liked Harvey," Nicholas said to it. "Anyway, I like you. I wish you were my hamster."

"And I wish those traps had worked," Father said, looking at his wastebaskets. "I can't understand what went wrong." He picked up the now wilted lettuce leaves and threw them away. Nicholas put the blocks back in his room. Mother folded up the towels again.

"I don't know about you," she said, turning on the lamps in the living room, "but I'm exhausted. I am going to play myself some relaxing music." She sat down at the piano and turned the pages of her music book.

"A nocturne would do it," Father said, settling down to listen. Nicholas turned his head.

"A what?" he asked. Where had he heard that word before?

"A nocturne is a piece of night music, dreamy, cloudy kind of music. The word 'nocturne' has to do with night."

"Then that's what Tony meant," Nicholas cried, jumping up. "And that's why Harvey sleeps all day and plays all night. All hamsters do. They're nocturnal!"

He rushed into the dark kitchen, where, sure enough, the new hamster had awakened and was running furiously around Harvey's exercise wheel, just as Harvey used to do at night.

"Now is the time to look for Harvey," Nicholas shouted, running up the stairs to his room. He tiptoed over to his bed and sat down in the dark. Everything was very quiet. Then downstairs his mother started playing the nocturne—very softly. It sounded very nocturnal indeed. Nicholas listened, but he was also listening for something else—for the sound of a hamster waking up to play. What kind of sound would that be?

Then he heard it. A rustle and a scratch. And another rustle and another scratch! It came from underneath his bookshelf! Nicholas turned on his lamp, just in time to see Harvey's pink nose poking out from the tiniest crack between the bookshelf and the wall!

Nicholas waited until Harvey had squeezed himself out into the room, and then he swooped down and picked him up.

"I've got him!" he called to his parents, and ran downstairs.

"Good for you," Father said. "That's the way to hunt hamsters!"

"I never thought I'd consider a hamster so absolutely beautiful," said Mother, patting the top of Harvey's head with one finger. "How did you like my hamster music, Harvey?"

Then Nicholas put Harvey back in his cage. The two hamsters stared at each other for a moment. Then the new hamster returned to the exercise wheel and Harvey began to eat.

Nicholas and his parents watched them, and Nicholas began to feel a strange feeling of wildest hope. He looked at his mother and father. Did he dare to ask?

"Do you think…" he began, "…if I took very good care of him…that maybe…?" His mother and father nodded, almost together.

"Yes," his father said. "You're an expert on hamsters. I don't see why you shouldn't have one of your own."

"Yes," agreed Nicholas's mother. "I rather like hamsters now. We'll get him a cage in the morning. Tonight he can sleep in a plastic wastebasket."

Just then the doorbell rang. It was Tony. He had come to fetch Harvey. He was very surprised to see another white hamster in Harvey's cage. Nicholas took his new hamster out, and it ran up his arm to sit on his shoulder.

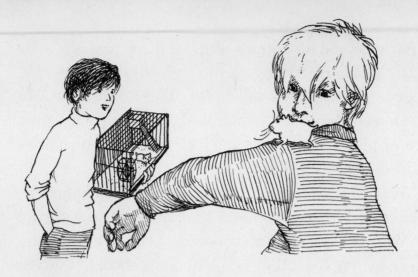

"Hey," Tony said. "How come you got a hamster?
It's not your birthday or anything, is it?"

Nicholas shook his head. "No," he said happily. "It
was just by accident."

Tony was puzzled. "Oh," was all he said, as if he
understood. But he didn't. He picked up Harvey's cage
and the bags of food and shavings. "Well, thanks a lot
for taking care of Harvey for me."

Nicholas went with him to the door. "You're wel-
come," he said. "See you tomorrow."

In the mirror next to the front door, Nicholas saw
himself with his hamster. The hamster was sitting on
Nicholas's head. It looked very happy up there, and
underneath it Nicholas looked happy, too.